MW00761706

To: _____

**With loads of love,
Gpa & Oma**

From: _____

To my nephew, Vito ~ S. R.

tiger tales
5 River Road, Suite 128, Wilton, CT 06897
This edition published in the United States 2020
First published in the United States 2006
Originally published in Great Britain 2006
by Little Tiger Press Ltd.
Text and illustrations copyright © 2006, 2020 Little Tiger Press Ltd.
ISBN-13: 978-1-68010-466-0 • ISBN-10: 1-68010-466-7
Printed in China • LTP/1800/3098/1219
All rights reserved • 10 9 8 7 6 5 4 3 2

For more insight and activities, visit us at www.tigertalesbooks.com

Twinkle, Twinkle, Twinkle, Little Star

and other favorite
bedtime rhymes

Illustrated by Sanja Rešček

tiger tales

Star Light, Star Bright

Star light, star bright,
First star I see tonight,
I wish I *may*, I wish I *might*,
Have the wish I wish tonight.

Wee Willie Winkle

Wee Willie Winkle runs
through the town,
Upstairs and downstairs,
in his nightgown.
Rapping at the window, crying through the lock:
"Are the children in their beds, for now it's eight o'clock?"

Are You Sleeping?

Are you sleeping,
Are you sleeping?
Brother John,
Brother John?
Morning bells are ringing,
Morning bells are ringing.
Ding, ding, dong.
Ding, ding, dong.

Jack Be Nimble

Jack be nimble,
Jack be quick.
Jack jump over
the candlestick.

Hush, Little Baby

Hush, little baby, don't say a word,
Papa's gonna buy you a mockingbird.

And if that mockingbird won't sing,
Papa's gonna buy you a diamond ring.

And if that diamond ring turns brass,
Papa's gonna buy you a looking glass.

And if that looking glass gets broke,
Papa's gonna buy you a billy goat.

And if that billy goat won't pull,
Papa's gonna buy you a cart and bull.

And if that cart and bull turn over,
Papa's gonna buy you a dog named Rover.

And if that dog named Rover won't bark,
Papa's gonna buy you a horse and cart.

And if that horse and cart fall down,
You'll still be the sweetest little baby in town.

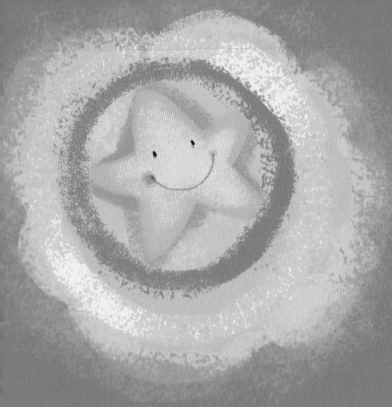

Twinkle, Twinkle, Little Star

Twinkle, twinkle, little star,
How I wonder what you are.
Up above the world so high,
Like a diamond in the sky.
Twinkle, twinkle, little star,
How I wonder what you are.

Diddle, Diddle, Dumpling

Diddle, diddle, dumpling, my son John
Went to bed with his stockings on.
One shoe off and one shoe on,
Diddle, diddle, dumpling,
my son John.

Teddy Bear, Teddy Bear

Teddy bear, teddy bear,
touch your nose.

Teddy bear, teddy bear,
touch your toes.

Teddy bear, teddy bear,
turn around.

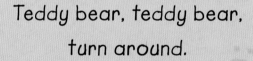

Teddy bear, teddy bear,
touch the ground.

Teddy bear, teddy bear,
go upstairs.

Teddy bear, teddy bear,
say your prayers.

Teddy bear, teddy bear,
turn off the light.

Teddy bear, teddy bear,
say good night.

It's Raining, It's Pouring

It's raining, it's pouring,
The old man is snoring.
He went to bed
    and bumped his head,
And couldn't get up
    in the morning.

Rock-a-Bye, Baby

Rock-a-bye, baby, in the treetop.

When the wind blows, the cradle will rock.

When the bough breaks, the cradle will fall,

And down will come baby, cradle and all.

Goosey, Goosey, Gander

Goosey, Goosey, Gander
Whither shall I wander?
Upstairs and downstairs,
And in my lady's chamber.

There I met an old man,
Who wouldn't say his prayers,
I took him by the left leg,
And led him down the stairs.

Old King Cole

Old King Cole was a merry old soul,
And a merry old soul was he.
He called for his pipe,
And he called for his bowl,
And he called for his fiddlers three.

Hey, Diddle, Diddle

Hey, diddle, diddle,
The cat and the fiddle,
The cow jumped
Over the moon;
The little dog laughed
To see such fun,
And the dish ran away
With the spoon.

Humpty Dumpty

Humpty Dumpty sat on a wall,
Humpty Dumpty had a great fall.
All the King's horses,
and all the King's men,
Couldn't put Humpty
together again.

Pat-a-Cake

Pat-a-cake, pat-a-cake,
baker's man,
Bake me a cake as fast
as you can.
Roll it and pat it and mark it
with a B,
And put it in the oven
for baby and me.

Jack and Jill

Jack and Jill went up the hill
To fetch a pail of water;
Jack fell down and broke his crown,
And Jill came tumbling after.

Mary, Mary, Quite Contrary

"Mary, Mary, quite contrary,
How does your garden grow?"
"With silver bells and cockleshells,
And pretty maids all in a row."

I See the Moon

I see the moon,
And the moon sees me.
God bless the moon,
And God bless me.

Come, Let's to Bed

"Come, let's to bed," says Sleepy Head.

"Wait a while," says Slow.

"Put on the pan," says Greedy Nan.

"We'll eat before we go."

Red Sky at Night

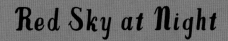

Red sky at night,
Shepherd's delight.
Red sky in morning,
Shepherds take warning.

Girls and Boys, Come Out to Play

Girls and boys,
come out to play,
The moon is shining
as bright as day.

Leave your supper
and leave your sleep,
And come with
your playfellows
into the street.

Now the Day Is Over

Now the day is over,
Night is drawing nigh,
Shadows of the evening
Steal across the sky.

Now the darkness gathers,
Stars begin to peep,
Birds and beasts and flowers
Soon will be asleep.

Matthew, Mark, Luke, and John

Matthew, Mark, Luke, and John,

Bless the bed that I lie on.

Four corners to my bed,

Four angels 'round my head.

One to watch and one to pray

And two to guide me through the day.

The Man in the Moon

The man in the moon
Looked out of the moon
And this is what he said,
"'Tis time that, now I'm getting up,
All babies went to bed."